Hip-Hop: A Short History

by C.F. Earl

Superstars of Hip-Hop

Alicia Keys

Beyoncé

Black Eyed Peas

Ciara

Dr. Dre

Drake

Eminem

50 Cent

Flo Rida

Hip Hop: A Short History

Jay-Z

Kanye West

Lil Wayne

LL Cool J

Ludacris

Mary J. Blige

Notorious B.I.G.

Rihanna

Sean "Diddy" Combs

Snoop Dogg

T.I.

T-Pain

Timbaland

Tupac

Usher

Hip-Hop: A Short History

by C.F. Earl

Mason Crest

Hip-Hop: A Short History

Mason Crest
370 Reed Road
Broomall, Pennsylvania 19008
www.masoncrest.com

Printed and bound in the United States of America.

First printing
9 8 7 6 5 4 3 2 1

Library of Congress Cataloging-in-Publication Data

Earl, C. F.
Hip-hop : a short history / by C.F. Earl.
p. cm. – (Superstars of hip hop)
Includes index.
ISBN 978-1-4222-2519-6 (hardcover) – ISBN 978-1-4222-2508-0 (series hardcover) – ISBN 978-1-4222-9221-1 (ebook)
1. Rap (Music)—History and criticism—Juvenile literature. 2. Hip-hop—Juvenile literature. I. Title.
ML3531.E27 2012
782.42164909–dc22
2011005805

Produced by Harding House Publishing Services, Inc.
www.hardinghousepages.com
Interior Design by MK Bassett-Harvey.
Cover design by Torque Advertising & Design.

Publisher's notes:

- All quotations in this book come from original sources and contain the spelling and grammatical inconsistencies of the original text.
- The Web sites mentioned in this book were active at the time of publication. The publisher is not responsible for Web sites that have changed their addresses or discontinued operation since the date of publication. The publisher will review and update the Web site addresses each time the book is reprinted.

Contents

Hip-Hop lingo

Rap is a kind of music where rhymes are chanted, often with music in the background. When people are rapping, they make up these rhymes, sometimes off the top of their heads.

Riffs are musical phrases that are often made up while musicians are playing.

Chapter 1

The Roots of Hip-Hop

Life is full of rhythms. The tap of heels on the sidewalk . . . the drip of rain on the roof . . . the beating of a heart. These rhythms are everywhere.

The world we live in is also filled with words. They can be angry or happy. They can be sad or proud. You can use words to tell others how you feel. You can use words to tell a story. Words, like the rhythms of life, are everywhere. And they can be used in many different ways.

Hip-hop music mixes the rhythms and words. Rappers use their words to express how they feel. They tell stories. Then they add rhythm to the words. Hip-hop beats can make you want to dance. The rhythm of the music can make you tap your toe. It can make you nod your head.

Today, hip-hop is one of the most popular types of music. You can hear hip-hop on the radio and on TV. Hip-hop is played all over the world. But hip-hop is more than just music. Hip-hop is in clothing and art. It's in dance and movies. It's a way of thinking about life.

From Africa to America

Hip-hop was born in America. But hip-hop's roots stretch all the way across the Atlantic Ocean to Africa. The sounds of Africa could be heard in the earliest hip-hop. And today, traditional African music is still a big part of hip-hop. Drums and rhythm have always been at the heart of African music. Those rhythms are also in hip-hop. Sing-alongs are another part of African music hip-hop has carried on.

Hip-hop's history in America starts with slavery. Slavery was terrible. Africans were taken from their homes. They were put in ships and sent to other places far away. They were bought and sold. Then they were forced to work for slave owners. The Africans were treated like things instead of people.

But Africans never gave up. They found ways to stay connected with their home. Music was one way they stayed strong.

Blacks would sing while they worked. They sang about being free. They sang about Africa and about their lives. Blacks sang in groups and on their own. The rhythm of their work gave the songs their beat. Through music, they could rise above their pain. And music helped bring African Americans together. Music gave blacks a way to get their feelings out and share them.

White people tried to take away what made Africans human. By keeping the music of Africa alive, blacks held on to it.

The Rhythm of Worship

Many Africans became Christians in the United States. But they made the faith their own in many ways. Rhythm and singing became a big part of worship. Sometimes, preaching and singing mixed together.

In black churches, ministers used "call-and-response" in their preaching. The minister might shout a question to his church.

Then the people would shout out an answer. This back-and-forth would find its way to hip-hop music.

The great African American minister Martin Luther King Jr. spoke of "singing the Word." In the 1960s, King led the civil rights movement. Like many black preachers, King used rhythm in his speaking. His voice rose and fell, loud, then soft. He stretched some words out until they sounded like music.

Church has always been important to African Americans. Many popular singers, including hip-hop artists, got their starts as members of a church choir. Gospel music has also influenced other styles of music, including R&B and soul.

Gospel singing was also a big part of worship in African American churches. Often, the preacher's words and the music from gospel singers wove together. In black churches, music, spoken words, and rhythm were mixed.

Church wasn't the only place to hear African American music. In the days after slavery, black music could be heard in the streets and in dance halls. Before long, talented artists made the music famous. They also helped form new types of American music. And all the while, they kept the sounds of Africa alive.

Rhythm and Blues

The blues was a type of music that came from the songs slaves sang. The blues was also about getting out a person's pain and sadness in a song.

In the 1940s, blues was mixed with a music called jazz. Jazz was another form of African American music. It became popular across the country in the 1920s. Together, blues and jazz became Rhythm and Blues (R&B). In the 1950s, R&B helped to shape early rock and roll.

R&B musicians loved drums. They were masters of the "shuffle" rhythm. A "shuffle" is a pair of notes that are repeated. The first beat is stronger. The second beat is less strong. The shuffle shaped a lot of blues and early rock and roll.

The Godfather of Hip-Hop

James Brown was born in 1933. He was born in the South during the Depression, when many people were poor. Many people were out of work. Things were even worse for African Americans. Black people were kept from being completely equal to whites. African Americans were treated like they weren't as good as whites.

Born and raised amid poverty and segregation, James Brown used his voice to give hope to others with similar backgrounds. His many nicknames—"Soul Brother Number One," "the Godfather of Soul," and "the Godfather of Hip-Hop"—show his influence and importance on the music scene.

Times were tough for James Brown growing up, but he found a way to help all African Americans rise above trouble. During the 1960s, Brown helped make soul music popular. Soul mixed gospel and R&B. Many people started calling James Brown "Soul Brother Number One" and "the Godfather of Soul."

Fans loved soul music because it was fun. It also came with a powerful message. James Brown recorded songs with titles like "Say It Loud—I'm Black and I'm Proud." The Godfather of Soul helped to spread the idea that "Black is beautiful!" Across America, Brown told his fans they should be proud of who they are.

James Brown's singing mixed blues, gospel, jazz, and other styles. He was one of the great singers in American music. The way he sang shaped many singers' styles that came after him. But Brown didn't just sing. He danced, swung the microphone, stomped the rhythm. He'd jump as high as he could. Then he'd land on his knees. Brown put on a great show.

Though many know James Brown as the Godfather of Soul, he also helped build hip-hop. In many ways, James Brown was the Godfather of Hip-Hop too! Few artists have had as much of an effect on popular music as James Brown.

Soul music helped set the stage for the hip-hop artists **rapping** in the 1970s and '80s. But before then, another form of music came out. Funk music, like soul, also helped shape hip-hop.

Funk Music

Funk music had fancy rhythms but simple songs. They were often built around one or two **riffs** (short groups of notes).

Funk was meant for dancing. Funk musicians wanted people to feel the beat so much that they couldn't help but dance! The bass guitar played a big role in funk music. The bass was played louder in funk than in any music before it. With its loud bass and dance-ready beats, funk paved the way for hip-hop.

When hip-hop started, it took lots of pieces from other kinds of black music. It took pieces from African Americans' past—both good and bad—and remade it into something new and amazing.

Hip-Hop lingo

DJ is short for disc jockey. A DJ plays music on the radio or at a party and announces the songs.

A **turntable** is the part of a phonograph (record player) that holds the plastic record and turns around under the needle. Sometimes a record player is called a turntable, too.

MC is short for master of ceremonies, the person who acts as the host for an entertainment program.

Chapter 2

The Birth of Hip-Hop

When he was twelve, Clive Campbell moved from Jamaica to New York City's South Bronx with his family. Campbell was a big kid, so friends called him Hercules. In the early 1970s, Campbell began to **DJ** at parties. He used the name Kool Herc when he DJ'd.

Herc and another DJ, DJ Hollywood, brought a Jamaican-style of dance music to the Bronx. It was called cutting and mixing. It took one small part of a song and played it again and again until it became a new piece of music. Kool Herc took two copies of the same record and put each on one of his two **turntables**. First, he'd play a short drum part from the song (called a "break") using one turntable. Then, he'd switch to the other record to play the same drum part after the first was done. By switching back and forth between the records, he could turn a short drum part into a whole new song.

While Kool Herc was on his turntables, he'd also **MC**. Using a microphone, he'd talk over the music he was playing. He'd mix in jokes, boasts, or urge people to dance. This was the beginning of adding rap to hip-hop. Today, rapping is a huge part of hip-hop music and hip-hop culture.

Soon, Herc's parties became more famous. The parties were recorded and passed around New York on cassette tapes. With more people hearing Herc's style of DJing, more DJs could add to his sound.

Afrika Bambaataa was one of the most important of these DJs. Bambaataa mixed in sounds from rock and roll and even television shows. He added his own flavor to Herc's sound. Bambaataa and Herc liked to compete against each other to see who was the best DJ. The two friends set up their turntables in city parks. Then, they'd DJ while fans watched. Each wanted to prove he could DJ better than the other.

Soon more DJs and rappers came along. Artists like Grandmaster Flash, the Lost Poets, and Grandmaster Caz with the Cold Crush Brothers all added to Kool Herc's style of music. Grandmaster Caz was the first DJ to start rhyming over the music from his turntables. He helped to bring rap into hip-hop music for the first time. The Lost Poets used hip-hop to talk about politics.

Hip-hop gave young African Americans a voice. Hip-hop could be whatever they wanted it to be. It couldn't be held down by rules. MCs could rhyme about anything they wanted. They could swear. They could make jokes. They could express anger or happiness. But, most of all, they could be themselves.

But hip-hop was more than just music. Hip-hop had its own language, fashion, and art. In the 1970s, graffiti became the image of hip-hop.

Graffiti

In the early 1970s, a mail deliveryman named Vic set a goal for himself. He wanted to ride every subway and bus in New York City. But he needed a way to keep track of the buses and trains he'd been on. So he started writing his name and job number (156) on each one he rode. "Vic 156" started to show up all over the city.

A young messenger named Demetrius (who lived on 183rd Street in New York) was also leaving his mark on subway cars. He'd write Taki 183 on the insides and outsides of subway cars. Kids all over the city started to do the same thing. Soon, lots of kids were "tagging" different buildings and subway cars. They wanted to see their own tag in as many different places as possible.

Hip-hop is more than music—it is a culture. Part of the cultural expression is through graffiti. Subway cars were favorite targets for graffiti artists. What began as "tagging" something just with initials or a symbol became an art form of complex, colorful images.

It didn't take long for graffiti to become more than tagging. Graffiti artists started to work with different kinds of styles. They added more color and tried to create more images. Graffiti was becoming an art style all its own.

Artists began using spray paint to create bigger pieces in less time. They needed to get their art up quickly before they were caught. Graffiti was beautiful and creative—but it was still against the law. Graffiti became more and more popular anyway. Soon, it was all over the subways of New York City. Then, artists in Philadelphia and other cities spread graffiti all over the country.

Break-dancers entertained club crowds during "get-down" sections of the music. Martial arts and Latino dances added their influences to the "drop" and "in and out" moves. Before long, crowds on the streets were introduced to these young people spinning their bodies in almost unbelievable ways.

Some people saw graffiti as something ugly. They thought it was a sign of cities falling apart. But for artists and those who loved their work, graffiti was a beautiful thing. It gave a look to hip-hop's sound. It helped inspire DJs and MCs. Over time, graffiti became hip-hop's own art form.

Breaking

Kool Herc's DJing shaped the sounds of early hip-hop. The way he turned the "break" of a song into new music brought the new music a lot of fans. Herc's "breakbeats" drew artists and musicians to hip-hop.

Another big part of hip-hop culture during the 1970s and early '80s was breaking. Breaking was a type of dancing that fans of breakbeats created. These dancers called themselves "break-boys" or "b-boys." Breaking was also called b-boying or break dancing.

Like graffiti, breaking added to the music of hip-hop. It gave fans something to watch while listening to a DJ or MC. It also gave hip-hop fans a dance style all their own. Breaking mixed moves from Latino dances and Asian martial arts with new moves. B-boys had their own breaking clubs. There dancers could get together to see who could break best.

Graffiti artists shaped the look of hip-hop. MCs and DJs gave hip-hop its sound and music. B-boys created hip-hop's dance moves. In the early days of hip-hop, these three parts were closely connected. Hip-hop life was made up of music, art, and dance. Often, hip-hop fans loved all three. A b-boy dancing in a club might tag a wall with his name. DJs and MCs in the South Bronx would break as well as make music. Graffiti artists could be using a spray can one minute, and a microphone the next.

Hip-hop gave young people living in big cities a way to express themselves. It gave young black kids a way to get out their feelings. Now they could celebrate who they were. Hip-hop told young people, "Your voice can be heard. Your name counts. Your rhythm is powerful."

Hip-Hop lingo

Bootleg refers to recordings put out without official permission.
Singles are songs that are sold by themselves.
Synthesizers use computer electronic technology to produce and manage sound.

Chapter 3

Growing Strong

Hip-hop was too strong to stay within the streets of the Bronx. Before long, hip-hop was spreading across the country. In California, new artists added their ideas to hip-hop. Hip-hop's voice was growing louder.

Hip-hop was growing up. New artists started to record music. More and more people were starting to take hip-hop seriously.

Zulu Nation

In 1974, Afrika Bambaataa (also known as Bam) started a group of DJs, graffiti artists, and break-dancers. He called his group the Universal Zulu Nation.

Bambaataa had led a gang called the Black Spades. After going to Africa on a trip, Bambaataa changed his mind on a lot of things. He decided that the Black Spades weren't doing the things he wanted to be doing. He wanted to help make things better for the Bronx. He wanted to change things. He thought hip-hop could help.

The Universal Zulu Nation started bringing people together to help others. They held neighborhood cleanups and block parties. They held classes and organized speeches. They had canned-food drives and started teaching programs for young people. Afrika Bambaataa and the Zulu Nation crew showed people that hip-hop could be used to change the world.

The First Hip-Hop Records

By the end of the 1970s, graffiti crews were tagging subway cars, buildings, and streetlights. B-boys had moved from dancing on the street to dancing in clubs. DJs and MCs like the Cold Crush Brothers and the Treacherous Three started performing with a smooth, showy style.

Hip-hop was becoming very popular. But there were still no recordings of the new music except for **bootleg** tapes. These tapes might be recorded at a concert and then passed between friends. Hip-hop wasn't on the radio yet, but you could hear it coming out of boom boxes walking down the street.

The Fatback Band and the Sugarhill Gang were the first rappers to put out records of their music. The Sugarhill Gang's "Rapper's Delight" became a hit overnight. The song was played on the radio and started selling a lot of copies very quickly.

The b-boys, artists and DJs that helped start hip-hop finally heard their music on the radio. Not everyone liked "Rapper's Delight." Not everyone who loved hip-hop thought the song was "real hip-hop." But it was a start. Finally, hip-hop was on the radio.

Rappers and DJs saw the Sugarhill Gang's success and wanted to follow their path. They started recording their own **singles**.

The hip-hop culture was becoming less and less underground. It wasn't just for a few people anymore. Hip-hop was for everyone to enjoy. Once hip-hop was played on the radio, people who'd never heard it before had a chance to understand what it was. Hip-hop was spreading across the country. It was leaving behind bootlegs and DJ parties for bigger success. Hip-hop was growing and changing.

The Growth of Dance

While hip-hop's music was becoming more popular, breaking was also making itself known. Charlie Robot was the first to show "Ro-

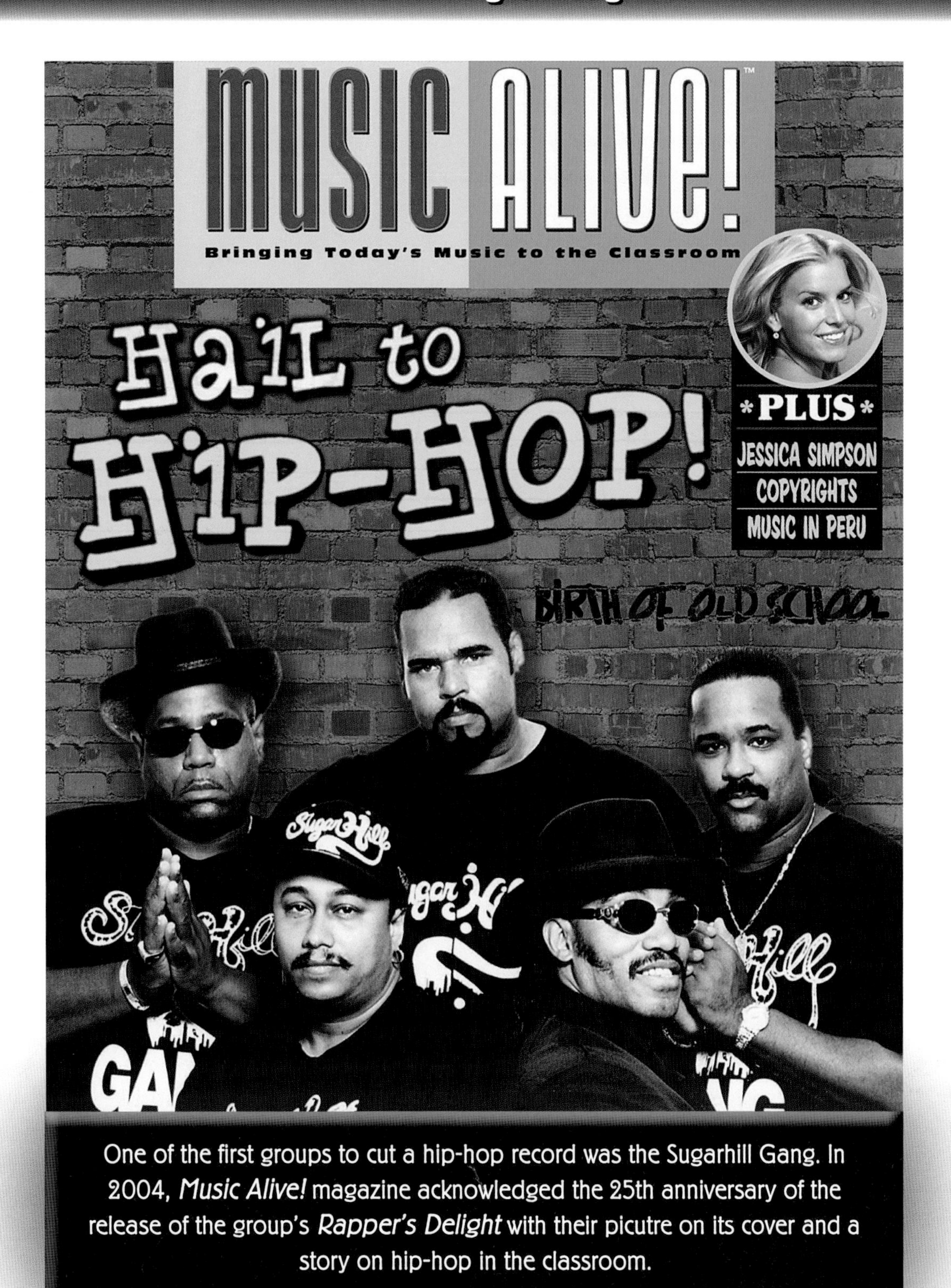

One of the first groups to cut a hip-hop record was the Sugarhill Gang. In 2004, *Music Alive!* magazine acknowledged the 25th anniversary of the release of the group's *Rapper's Delight* with their picutre on its cover and a story on hip-hop in the classroom.

Hip-hop made its way to television and film, and its influence could not be ignored. It became a category for many music and video awards. Here, Crazy Legs and the Rock Steady Crew—pioneers in hip-hop dance—are shown at the 2005 *VH1 Hip-Hop Honors.*

bot" dance moves to America on the TV show *Soul Train*. New b-boy groups were forming, too. Uprock, Breakmachine, the Rock Steady Crew, and others were all coming together to break. Breakers were coming up with moves like popping and locking. B-girls began stepping out as well. Dancers like Headspin Janet, Lady Doze, and Daisy "Baby Love" Castro were showing that women could break as well as—and sometimes better than—the b-boys.

Dancers would compete to see who the best dancer was. The battles between breakers could start or end friendships. A single battle could make or break a dancer's reputation.

Hip-Hop's Rise

By the early 1980s, America couldn't ignore hip-hop. TV talk-show hosts like David Letterman asked b-boys to perform on their shows. The group Funky 4 + 1 performed on *Saturday Night Live*. Hip-hop even had its own movies when *Breakin'* and *Breakin' 2: Electric Boogaloo* came out. Breaking crews, MCs, and DJs were becoming stars.

White musicians like the Beastie Boys and Blondie's Debbie Harry were also watching hip-hop. It wasn't long before these artists were trying to match the sound of the music. Hip-hop had its first television show with *Graffiti Rock*. Special guests like Run-D.M.C., Kool Moe Dee, and Special K went on the show.

Rappers and DJs were also adding new ideas to hip-hop all the time. In 1982, Afrika Bambaataa used **synthesizers** and electronic drums on his album *Planet Rock*. Rappers were telling more stories in their rhymes. Scratching started to become more and more popular, thanks to artists like Grand Wizard Theodore. Grandmaster Flash's song "The Message" set a new standard for rappers. Flash rapped about the pressure of living in poor city neighborhoods. His lyrics were smart and catchy. "The Message" was about what life was really like, even if that truth was ugly.

DJs also started to use samplers. They'd take small parts from songs and mix them together to create new music. Some thought this sampling was stealing. But others saw that it was taking pieces of the past and making something new. Hip-hop was remaking popular music. It was taking old ideas and making them new again. With music, art, and dance, hip-hop was also reshaping the pop world.

Hip-Hop lingo

Mainstream music is music enjoyed by almost everyone.
An **album** is a group of songs collected together on a CD.

Chapter 4

Going Mainstream

In just a few years, hip-hop went from the streets to the movie screen. It changed the kind of music people listened to. It changed what people watched on TV. It wouldn't be long before everything from soft-drink commercials to pop music started taking on hip-hop's sound. Hip-hop had come a long way from the streets of New York's South Bronx.

In 1986, the Beastie Boys put out their single "(You Gotta) Fight for Your Right (To Party!)" The song moved to the top ten on the *Billboard* singles charts. An Aerosmith song, "Walk This Way," featured rap group Run-D.M.C. Like the Beastie Boys song, "Walk This Way" made it into the top ten on the charts. A female rap group called Salt-n-Pepa put out a single called "Push It." "Push It" made it into the top twenty on the charts.

MTV and Hip-Hop

MTV was created to play music videos. But the network was very slow to allow black artists' videos on the air. In the early 1980s, *Rolling Stone* magazine wrote that out of 750 videos shown on MTV, fewer than twenty-five were by black artists.

One man's music changed all that. Michael Jackson was one of the most popular artists in the 1980s. But MTV still wouldn't play Jackson's videos. CBS Records president Walter Yetnikoff called MTV. He told them that if they didn't play Jackson, they'd never get another video from the company. MTV saw that they couldn't keep black artists off their network. They started showing Michael Jackson's video, and he became an even bigger star.

Jackson opened up MTV for other black artists, too. Prince, Run-D.M.C., the Fat Boys, Salt-n-Pepa, and others were all able to get their videos on MTV after Jackson. Once hip-hop made it onto MTV, people all over America could hear it. People could also see the clothes artists wore and the dance moves that they used.

"Pop Rap"

Some hip-hop fans felt the music was changing too much. They thought that many artists weren't making "real" hip-hop anymore. Some fans worried that the music they loved was being taken over by people who didn't really understand it. Other fans just didn't know what to think about the new "pop rap." Could hip-hop keep its history and change at the same time? Could hip-hop be cool when everyone listened to it?

Some hip-hop fans didn't like that white musicians were starting to come into hip-hop. Many believed artists like Vanilla Ice and Marky Mark Wahlberg were using hip-hop. These white artists, some said, were just trying to make money by doing what was popular. Some hip-hop fans thought they didn't even understand the music or what it meant.

With the Beastie Boys, however, things were different. They didn't try to be something they weren't. Their songs expressed who they were. They added to the voice of hip-hop. They didn't try to steal someone else's voice. Their hit "(You Gotta) Fight For

Your Right (to Party)" made them famous. And their music wasn't viewed in the same way as other white rap artists'.

Hip-hop's goal had always been to reach as many people as possible. But now, some people thought it was becoming too **mainstream**.

Hip-Hop in Every Home

More and more people were listening to hip-hop. It was on the radio. It was on TV. Before long, American businesses could see hip-hop was a way to reach young people. Companies like Coca-

When hip-hop entered the mainstream, white artists joined in, much to the anger of some hip-hop originators. One group—the Beastie Boys—did have the respect of many hip-hop artists. Why? They weren't trying to be black.

Cola, Pepsi, and Adidas wanted to make sure they got those young people's attention. And they knew they could do it with hip-hop.

In the 1980s, stars like Run-D.M.C., Kool Moe Dee, and Kurtis Blow all started working in commercials. The Fresh Prince (Will Smith) was in Mountain Dew ads on TV. Run-D.M.C. sold the Adidas shoes they wore. Appearing in ads was a way for artists to make money. But it was also a way to bring hip-hop to more people.

Once hip-hop was in commercials, it was reaching more people than ever. Even people who didn't listen to hip-hop now saw it on TV. They couldn't avoid it. Hip-hop was everywhere. The music and the lifestyle were now part of American life.

Women in early hip-hop were generally seen only as dancers or back-up singers. The first important female rap group was Salt-n-Pepa, shown here (left to right: DJ Sinderella [Deirdre Roper], Cheryl "Salt" James, and Sandy "Pepa" Denton). They helped open doors for other female musicians.

In 1988, the year's hip-hop record sales reached $100 million. Hip-hop had become good business. In 1989, *Billboard* magazine added rap song and **album** charts. That meant that rap would have its own place next to rock and pop. *Billboard* would track sales of albums and singles for the first time. MTV started a hip-hop TV show called *Yo! MTV Raps*. Soon, it was MTV's most popular show.

Women Find Their Place

Men had almost always been in charge in the world of hip-hop. Women were usually out of the spotlight. They were often made back-up singers or dancers. But by the end of the 1980s, female rappers were getting respect and attention for their own music.

Female rap groups rhymed about how men treated women. They rapped their demands to be treated equally. They also spoke about lifting up other women. They wanted to make all women feel good about themselves. Artists like Salt-n-Pepa and Monie Love wanted to give power to women through hip-hop.

True to Hip-Hop's Roots

In the 1980s, more and more rappers became political. Many rappers used their music to get out political messages. Groups like Public Enemy and Boogie Down were popular and political. Public Enemy's second album *It Takes a Nation of Millions to Hold Us Back* was a huge hit. Public Enemy's Chuck D. said that hip-hop was bigger than entertaining people. He said that hip-hop was a way to share ideas. It was a way to tell stories that aren't always heard.

Hip-hop was bigger than ever in the '80s. It had reached new fans and changed music. Hip-hop was on the radio and on TV. Hip-hop had come from the streets of the Bronx. Now, it was in every home in America. Hip-hop hadn't reached the height of its success yet. But it was getting closer all the time.

Hip-Hop lingo

Lyrics are the words in a song.
A **record label** is a company that produces and sells music.

Chapter 5

Hip-Hop Blows Up

Hip-hop had reached every corner of the country. Hits were played on TV and on the radio. New artists added new voices and ideas to the music. Hip-hop was on its way to becoming the most popular kind of music. But not everyone approved of hip-hop.

Gangsta Rap

In the 1980s, a new kind of rap came on the scene. Artists like rappers Scooly D and Ice T started rapping about living as a gangster. Guns, drugs, and sex were all a part of gangsta rap. Rap had always been about telling stories. With gangsta rap, artists were just telling different kinds of stories. The **lyrics** made some people mad. But they also brought hip-hop to more people than ever.

In 1988, the rap group N.W.A. put out *Straight Outta Compton*. It was one of the biggest hip-hop albums of all time. The album sold millions of copies. On *Straight Outta Compton*, N.W.A. rapped about the gangsta life in L.A. Their California sound and gangsta lyrics became very popular. N.W.A. made Los Angeles a new home for hip-hop. New York had always been the place for hip-hop. Now the West Coast had its own sound.

By the 1990s, many more gangsta rappers were putting out music. Soon, gangsta rap become the most popular kind of hip-hop music.

Many people didn't like the new form of rap. Politicians and religious leaders said the music was bad for young people. They said that gangsta rap was only about guns, violence, and drugs. They said that hip-hop had become a way to make these things cool. They thought the lyrics in gangsta rap went too far.

But gangsta rappers believed they were just making music. They said they didn't tell kids to go and do the things in their songs. They weren't trying to make the gang life cool. They were just telling stories about things that happened every day. In many places in America, the gangsta life was a reality. N.W.A. even called their music "reality rap."

Some rappers said they were just playing a character in their music. They said that their lyrics shouldn't be taken as the truth. They were using words to tell exciting stories, like in movies and TV shows. They said those other kinds of media had the same focus on violence, drugs, and sex that gansta rap did.

East Coast Against West Coast

In the early and mid 1990s, West Coast rap was becoming more and more popular. Artists like Dr. Dre, Snoop Dogg, and Tupac Shakur were the new hip-hop stars. L.A. **record label** Death Row Records was at the center of the West Coast rap scene. Death Row's head was Suge Knight

In 1993, Sean "Puff Daddy" Combs (now P. Diddy) started Bad Boy Records in New York. The label released rapper Notorious

Tupac Shakur, Snoop Dogg, and Suge Knight worked to make gangsta rap one of the most popular kinds of hip-hop in the 1990s.

B.I.G. in 1994. By 1995, Bad Boy and Death Row Records had become rivals. Tupac thought that Puffy and B.I.G. had set him up to be robbed and shot in 1994. Though B.I.G. and Puff said they had nothing to do with it, that didn't stop Tupac from thinking they were behind it.

Over the next few years, East and West Coast artists recorded songs dissing each other. Bad Boy and Death Row kept their battle going in songs and on stage. At the 1995 Source Awards, Death Row's Suge Knight called out Puffy and Bad Boy. It wasn't long before magazines and other media were talking about the East-against-West Coast rivalry. Some thought the media was taking advantage of hip-hop in order to make more money.

In September 1996, Tupac was shot and killed in Las Vegas. Six months later, Notorious B.I.G. was shot in Los Angeles. Hip-hop had lost two of its biggest stars. No one was sure if the deaths were tied together. But many people saw the loss of B.I.G. and Tupac as the end of the battle between the East and West Coast.

Artists came together to put an end to the rivalry. They saw that nothing good came of the fight. There have been many rivalries in hip-hop over the years. But none have been as well known or as tragic as the battle between coasts in the 1990s.

Hip-Hop Takes Over

By the mid 1990s, hip-hop was taking over music. Rap was one of the biggest selling kinds of music at the time. But hip-hop wasn't only taking over music. Hip-hop was also taking over business. Hip-hop artists were coming up with new ways to think about the music business.

Jay-Z was a rapper from Brooklyn, New York. In the early to mid-1990s, he was making music and trying to get a record deal. Soon, he met Damon Dash. Jay and Dash tried to get Jay on lots of different record labels. But it was no use. Everyone said they didn't want to sign Jay-Z.

Jay and Dash had an idea. They would start their own label. Together, they founded Roc-A-Fella Records. They started recording and selling Jay's music themselves. Then, when Jay became more popular, they went back to the labels that turned them down. With Roc-A-Fella, they had control over Jay's music. They also had more power to talk to the labels. They didn't need the labels anymore. They had their own. Today, many artists begin their own labels. They control their own music and bring up new artists.

Hip-hop was changing the way the music business worked. But it was also changing fashion in the 1990s. No matter who you were, hip-hop shaped the clothes you wore. Hip-hop's baggy jeans and big t-shirts became the cool thing to wear. Young people across the country dressed like their favorite hip-hop artists.

Hip-hop artists also started their own clothing companies. Jay-Z and Damon Dash started RocaWear. Jay and Dash knew that young people wanted to be just like the rappers they loved. The two men saw that hip-hop had always been more than music. They understood it was a style. And young people from all over the country wanted to get some of Jay-Z's style. By buying RocaWear, fans could feel even closer to the artist. Soon, P. Diddy started Sean Jean clothing. The Wu Tang Clan started Wu Wear.

Fashion was just one part of hip-hop's becoming a big business. Artists now had control over their own record labels and clothing companies. They could run things the way they wanted. They could make decisions for themselves.

Hip-Hop Branches Out

By the end of the 1990s, more hip-hop music was being made than ever before. Artists from all over the country were getting in on rap and hip-hop. Artists in Atlanta, New Orleans, Chicago, and Detroit were all making their mark on the music. Southern rap was beginning to become more popular.

More people than ever were buying and listening to hip-hop. Rappers were the new businessmen. They set fashion trends. Hip-hop had become a major part of American life.

Hip-Hop lingo

Charities are groups that give time, money, or other things to help make people's lives better.

Chapter 6

Hip-Hop and Modern Culture

Hip-hop has always been a blend of rhythm, voice, images, and movement. Today's hip-hop culture is still crossing lines and bringing more people together. Hip-hop is also more open than ever. No matter who you are, hip-hop has a place for you. Anyone can join in. In modern life, hip-hop is a part of politics, fashion, business, and charity.

Hip-Hop and Politics

In June 2004, the National Hip-Hop Political Convention was held in Newark, New Jersey. The convention was set up so that civil rights leaders could talk with hip-hop artists and fans. The group talked about how to use music to bring political change. Everyone who went to the convention wanted to get young people involved in politics. Most of all, though, they wanted hip-hop to be part of politics in America.

Today, many hip-hop activists want to use music to reach young people. They want to get more people into politics through hip-hop. Hip-hop has always had the power to move people. It's always been a way to share messages and ideas. In the twenty-first century, many people believe that hip-hop getting into politics is just the next step.

Hip-Hop and Religion

Just as hip-hop has moved into politics, it's also moved into religion. MTV.com wrote that hip-hop had become one of the most religious musical cultures. A new breed of religious artists raps about faith and their beliefs.

Many of these rappers are Christian, but rap doesn't have just one faith. There are Muslim, Jewish, and Hindu rappers. In the 2000s, Jewish musician Matisyahu's song "King Without A Crown" became a hit. Matisyahu's music mixed reggae and hip-hop with traditional Jewish beliefs.

In the 1980s, artists began releasing gospel rap. They mixed the sounds of church with the sound of the street. Today, Christian hip-hop has reached more people than ever. There are even awards for Christian hip-hop music.

Many modern Christian churches see hip-hop as a powerful way to speak to people. Some churches use rap and hip-hop dance in their services. They want to show people that their faith can be modern.

Religious rap hasn't always been as successful as nonreligious rap. But more people than ever are listening and making religious hip-hop music. Hip-hop has always been about giving people a voice. Today, many different voices can be heard in the religious hip-hop world.

"Hip-Hop Won't Stop"

In February 2005, the Smithsonian Institute said they would create a new exhibit about the history of hip-hop. The Smithsonian called the exhibit "Hip-Hop Won't Stop: The Beat, The Rhymes,

The Life." The exhibit was shown at the Smithsonian National Museum of American History in Washington, D.C.

Rappers, DJs, and producers all gave important items to the exhibit. Grandmaster Flash gave the exhibit two turntables he'd used. Yo! MTV Raps host Fab 5 Freddy gave a boom box. Pictures, album covers, and recordings were all part of the exhibit, too.

The Smithsonian's exhibit shows how far the culture has come. Hip-hop culture has truly become part of American culture.

Using Hip-Hop to Change the World

In 2001, Russell Simmons from Run-D.M.C. started the Hip-Hop Summit Action Network (HSAN). Simmons has been a big part of hip-hop music and business. With Run-D.M.C., he brought the music to more people than hip-hop had ever touched. With HSAN, Simmons wanted to make sure hip-hop was doing its part to help young people. HSAN's mission is to support young people using hip-hop. HSAN also wants to help create the next generation of American leaders.

The group works on many issues that are important to America's youth. HSAN works to make education better and keep kids in school. Its members sign up young people to vote. HSAN has also stood up for hip-hop as an art form. Russell Simmons and HSAN believe hip-hop can help change the world.

In the modern hip-hop culture, giving back is very important. Many artists set up their own charities. Rappers like Ludacris, P. Diddy, T.I., and many others have charities. These groups work on issues that are important to the artists and to the hip-hop world. Nelly's charity educates people about leukemia. The Ludacris Foundation works to keep kids in school. Kanye West's charity

Rappers Kanye West and Jay-Z joined to perform as The Throne in 2011. The pair released *Watch the Throne* and toured together. *Watch the Throne* was a massive hit and showed hip-hop's continuing popularity.

teaches kids about making music. Today, using hip-hop to make the world a better place is a big part of the culture.

Hip-Hop Around the World

Hip-hop has traveled a long way from the streets of the South Bronx. In the twenty-first century, hip-hop can be heard in Japan, France, the Philippines, and many other countries. Many artists in other countries started out trying to sound like American rappers. It wasn't long before artists around the world made hip-hop their own. New styles mix hip-hop and other kinds of music. Reggaeton blends Latin music with hip-hop. Bongo Flava mixes hip-hop and traditional Tanzanian music.

Hip-hop has become a truly global voice. For many around the world, hip-hop allows people to say what they want. It allows them to speak up and express themselves. In France, England, Russia, Japan, and other countries all over the world, hip-hop is the music of young people. Today, hip-hop can be heard worldwide.

A New Generation

New artists are bringing new ideas to hip-hop all the time. Rappers like Kanye West, B.o.B., and Drake are bringing new feelings into rap. Gnarls Barkley has hit it big with their sound, mixing pop, hip-hop, and R&B. The Roots mix rock and roll, jazz, soul, and hip-hop in their music.

With the help of the Internet, many artists are reaching more people than ever. Even artists without a record deal are able to get their music to people online.

Today, hip-hop is everywhere. You don't have to be a certain type of person to love hip-hop. Hip-hop is for everyone!

1619	Slaves are first brought to the United States from Africa.
1920s	Jazz becomes popular in the United States.
1933	James Brown, the "Godfather of Soul," is born.
1940s	The blues combine with jazz to become rhythm and blues.
1970s	DJ Kool Herc pioneers the use of breaks, isolations, and repeats using two turntables; break dancing emerges at parties and in public places in New York City; graffiti artist Vic makes his mark in New York, sparking the act of tagging; hip-hop as a cultural movement begins in the Bronx, New York City.
1974	Hip-hop pioneer Afrika Bambaataa organizes the Universal Zulu Nation.
1976	Grandmaster Flash & the Furious Five pioneer hip-hop MCing and freestyle battles.
1982	Afrika Bambaataa introduces synthesizers and electric drum machine sounds on his album *Planet Rock*.
1984	*Graffiti Rock*, the first hip-hop television show, premieres.
1985	*Krush Groove*, a hip-hop film about Def Jam Recordings, is released featuring Run-D.M.C., Kurtis Blow, LL Cool J, and the Beastie Boys.
1986	Run-D.M.C. are the first rappers to appear on the cover of *Rolling Stone* magazine; "(You Gotta) Fight for Your Right (To Party!)" by the Beastie Boys goes to the top ten on *Billboard* charts.
1988	*Yo! MTV Raps* premieres on MTV; annual record sales of hip-hop music reach $100 million; Upper Hutt Posse releases *E Tu*, New Zealand's first album of pure hip-hop.

1989	First gangsta rap album is released by N.W.A.; *Billboard* adds rap charts to its magazines; DJ Jazzy Jeff & The Fresh Prince become the first hip-hop artists to win a Grammy Award.
1990s	Hip-hop is established in Europe.
1996	Just D and Infinite Mass win the Swedish version of the Grammys.
2001	Russell Simmons founds the Hip-Hop Summit Action Network.
2003	At the Detroit Hip-Hop Summit, over 17,000 youths commit to ongoing youth leadership development utilizing hip-hop on April 26; over 11,000 voters are registered at the Philadelphia Hip-Hop Summit on August 14.
2004	National Hip-Hop Political Convention is held in Newark, New Jersey.
2005	Kanye West appears on the cover of *Time* magazine.
2006	The Smithsonian Institute announces the launch of "Hip-Hop Won't Stop: The Beat, The Rhymes, The Life," a new hip-hop exhibit to be displayed at the Smithsonian's National Museum of American History in Washington, D.C.
2007	Hip-hop album sales continue to fall despite being a popular genre; no album goes platinum.
2010	Somali-Canadian rapper and singer K'naan's "Waving Flag" is chosen to be the anthem for the 2010 FIFA World Cup.
2012	At a Snoop Dogg and Dr. Dre concert, a projection of Tupac Shakur performs with Snoop Dogg.

In Books

Baker, Soren. *The History of Rap and Hip Hop*. San Diego, Calif.: Lucent, 2006.

Comissiong, Solomon W. F. *How Jamal Discovered Hip-Hop Culture*. New York: Xlibris, 2008.

Cornish, Melanie. *The History of Hip Hop*. New York: Crabtree, 2009.

Czekaj, Jef. *Hip and Hop, Don't Stop!* New York: Hyperion, 2010.

Haskins, Jim. *One Nation Under a Groove: Rap Music and Its Roots*. New York: Jump at the Sun, 2000.

Hatch, Thomas. *A History of Hip-Hop: The Roots of Rap*. Portsmouth, N.H.: Red Bricklearning, 2005.

Websites

Foundation of African Hip-Hop Culture Online
www.africanhiphop.com

Hip-Hop
www.hip-hop.com

Hip-Hop Summit Action Network
www.hsan.org

SOHH
www.sohh.com

Index

About the Author

C.F. Earl is a writer living and working in Binghamton, New York. Earl writes mostly on social and historical topics, including health, the military, and finances. An avid student of the world around him, and particularly fascinated with almost any current issue, C.F. Earl hopes to continue to write for books, websites, and other publications for as long as he is able.

Picture Credits

Catuffe/SIPA: p. 24
Death Row Records/NMI: p. 35
Kazuhiro Nogi/AFP/Getty Images: p. 32
KRT/NMI: pp. 11, 18, 20
NMI: p. 17, 29, 30
PictureArts/OBrien Productions: p. 9
PRNewsFoto/NMI: p. 23
Reuters/Mike Hutchings: p. 6
Robyn Mackenzie: p. 1
Sbulkey/Dreamstime.com: p. 38
Tsuni/iPhoto: p. 26
WENN Photos: p. 14
Zuma Press/Nancy Kaszerman: p. 42

To the best knowledge of the publisher, all other images are in the public domain. If any image has been inadvertently uncredited, please notify Harding House Publishing Services, Vestal, New York 13850, so that rectification can be made for future printings.